Dear Parent:

Here is a book by an American children's book superstar:
Tomie de Paola!

You may recognize his style of art from one of his many books—
Strega Nona (a Caldecott Honor book), *Tomie de Paola's Favorite
Nursery Rhymes* or *Charlie Needs a Cloak,* to name a few. Adults
and children both love his humorous, bright-colored drawings.

Tomie showed talent early on. He was named "best artist" by his
teachers and classmates. He made a promise to himself that he
would be an artist and draw pictures, particularly for books. Forty
years later he says that he can truthfully say he kept his promise.

While not every child will become a famous artist, every child
needs encouragement. Experts say that the best thing we can do as
parents is to provide an environment where children learn to read,
write and have fun doing these. With books, magazines and
newspapers, good talk and good listening around them, children
naturally learn language, its patterns and its power.

We hope you and your child will like what the author has called a
"prehistoric fairy tale."

Sincerely,

Elizabeth Isele
Executive Editor
Weekly Reader Books

WEEKLY READER CHILDREN'S BOOK CLUB PRESENTS

Little Grunt
and the
Big Egg

A Prehistoric Fairy Tale

Tomie dePaola

Holiday House
New York

To *David Rogers*, who loves dinosaurs

This book is a presentation of Weekly Reader Books. Weekly Reader
books offers book clubs for children from preschool through high
school. For further information write to: **Weekly Reader Books,**
4343 Equity Drive, Columbus, Ohio 43228.

Published by arrangement with Holiday House. Weekly Reader is a
federally reqistered trademark of Field Publications.

Library of Congress Cataloging-in-Publication Data
De Paola, Tomie.
Little Grunt and the big egg : a prehistoric fairytale / written
and illustrated by Tomie dePaola.—1st ed.
p.   cm.
Summary: When a dinosaur hatches from the egg that Little Grunt
brought home for dinner, Mama and Papa Grunt let him keep it as a
pet until it grows too big for their cave.
ISBN 0-8234-0730-6
[1. Dinosaurs—Fiction.   2. Pets—Fiction.   3. Cave dwellers—
—Fiction.]   I. Title.
PZ7.D439Li 1989
[E]—dc19   88-17009   CIP   AC
ISBN 0-8234-0730-6

Once upon a time, in a big cave, past the volcano on the left, lived the Grunt Tribe. There was Unca Grunt, Ant Grunt, Granny Grunt, Mama Grunt, and Papa Grunt. Their leader was Chief Rockhead Grunt. The smallest Grunt of all was Little Grunt.

One Saturday morning, Mama Grunt said to Little Grunt, "Little Grunt, tomorrow the Ugga-Wugga Tribe are coming for Sunday brunch. Could you please go outside and gather two dozen eggs?"

"Yes, Mama Grunt," said Little Grunt, and off he went.

At that time of year, eggs were hard to find. Little Grunt looked and looked. No luck. He was getting tired.

"What am I going to do?" he said to himself. "I can't find a single egg. I'll try one more place."

And it was a good thing that he did, because there, in the one more place, was the biggest egg Little Grunt had ever seen.

It was too big to carry. It was too far to roll. And besides, Little Grunt had to be very careful. Eggs break *very* easily.

Little Grunt thought and thought.

"I know," he said. He gathered some of the thick pointy leaves that were growing nearby. He wove them into a mat. Then he carefully rolled the egg on top of it. He pulled and pulled and pulled the egg all the way home.

"My goodness," said the Grunt Tribe. "Ooga, ooga, what an egg! That will feed us *and* the Ugga-Wuggas. And even the Grizzler Tribe. Maybe we should invite *them* to Sunday brunch, too."

"I'll be able to make that special omelet I've been wanting to," said Mama Grunt.

"Ooga, ooga! Yummy! Yummy!" said all the Grunts.

They put the egg near the hearth, and then they all
went to bed.

That night, by the flickering firelight, the egg began
to make noise. CLICK, CRACK went the egg. CLICK,
CRACK, CLUNK. A big piece fell to the floor. CLICK,
CRACK, CLUNK, PLOP. The egg broke in half, and
instead of the big egg sitting by the fire . . .

There was a baby dinosaur!

"Waaangh," cried the baby dinosaur. And all the Grunt Tribe woke up.

"Ooga, ooga!" they said. "What are we going to do?"

"There goes the brunch!" said Unca Grunt.

"What will the Ugga-Wuggas say?" said Ant Grunt.

"I bet I'm allergic to that thing," said Papa Grunt.

Chief Rockhead Grunt said, "All I know is it can't stay..."

But before he could finish, Little Grunt said, "May I keep him? Please? *Please?*"

"Every boy needs a pet," said Granny Grunt.

Some of the Grunts said yes. Some of the Grunts said no. But it was finally decided that Little Grunt could keep the baby dinosaur.

"Against my better judgment," mumbled Chief Rockhead Grunt.

"Oh, well, I suppose I can make pancakes for Sunday brunch," said Mama Grunt.

"I'm going to call him George," said Little Grunt.
Little Grunt and George became great pals.

But there was a problem. The cave stayed the same
size, but George didn't. He began to grow.

And GROW.

And GROW.
The cave got very crowded.

And there were other problems.
George wasn't housebroken.

George ate ALL the leaves off ALL the trees and
ALL the bushes ALL around the cave. But still he
was hungry.

George liked to play—rough. George stepped on things.

And when he sneezed—well, it was a disaster.

"Ooga, ooga! Enough is enough!" said the Grunts.

"Either that dinosaur goes, or I go," said Unca Grunt.

"I spend all day getting food for him," said Ant Grunt.

"Achoo!" said Papa Grunt. "I told you I was allergic to him."

"He stepped on all my cooking pots and broke them," said Mama Grunt.

"I guess it wasn't a good idea to keep him," said Granny Grunt. "How about a nice *little* cockroach. They make nice pets."

"I'm in charge here," said Chief Rockhead Grunt. "And I say, *That giant lizard goes!*"

"Ooga, ooga! Yes! Yes!" said all the Grunts.

"But you promised," said Little Grunt.

The next morning, Little Grunt took George away
from the cave, out to where he had found him in the
first place.

"Good-bye, George," said Little Grunt. "I'll sure
miss you."

"Waaargh," said George.

Big tears rolled down both their cheeks. Sadly, Little Grunt watched as George walked slowly into the swamp.

"I'll never see him again," sobbed Little Grunt.

The days and months went by, and Little Grunt still missed George. He dreamed about him at night and drew pictures of him by day.

"Little Grunt certainly misses that dinosaur," said Mama Grunt.

"He'll get over it," said Papa Grunt.

"It's nice and peaceful here again," said Ant and Unca Grunt.

"I still say a cockroach makes a nice pet," said Granny Grunt.

"Ooga, ooga. Torches out. Everyone in bed," said Chief Rockhead.

That night, the cave started to shake. The floor began to pitch, and loud rumblings filled the air.

"Earthquake!" cried the Grunts, and they rushed to the opening of the cave.

"No, it's not," said Granny Grunt. "Look! Volcano!"

And sure enough, the big volcano was erupting all over the place. Steam and rocks and black smoke shot out of the top. Around the cave, big rocks and boulders tumbled and bounced.

"We're trapped! We're trapped!" shouted the Grunts. "What are we going to do?"

"Don't ask me!" said Chief Rockhead. "I resign."

"Now we have no leader," cried Ant Grunt.

"Now we're really in trouble!" shouted Papa Grunt. The lava was pouring out of the volcano in a wide, flaming river and was heading straight for the cave.

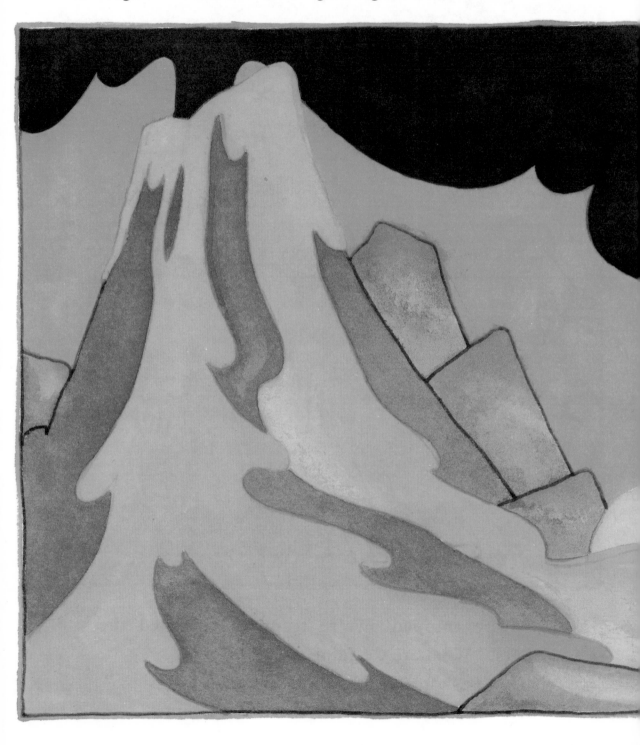

There wasn't enough time for the Grunts to escape.
All of a sudden, the Grunts heard a different noise.
"Waaargh! Wonk!"

"It's George," cried Little Grunt. "He's come to save us."

"Ooga, ooga! Quick!" said the Grunts as they all jumped on George's long neck and long back and long tail.

And before you could say Tyrannosaurus rex,

George carried them far away to safety.

"As your new leader," Papa Grunt said, "I say this is our new cave!"

"I like the kitchen," said Mama Grunt.

"Now, when I was the leader . . ." said Plain Rock-head Grunt.

"When do we eat?" said Unca Grunt.

"I can't wait to start decorating," said Ant Grunt.

"I always say a change of scenery keeps you from getting old," said Granny Grunt.

"And George can live right next door," said Little Grunt.

"Where is George?" asked Mama Grunt. "I haven't seen him all afternoon."

"Ooga, ooga. Here, George," called the Grunts.

"Waaargh," answered George.

"Look!" said Little Grunt.
"Oh no!" said the Grunts.
There was George, sitting on a pile of big eggs.

"I guess I'd better call George Georgina!"
said Little Grunt.

And they all lived happily ever after.